Japanese Fairy Tales

VOLUME 2

Stories by Keisuke Nishimoto
Illustrations by Yoko Imoto

HEIAN

© 1997 Text by Keisuke Nishimoto / Illustrations by Yoko Imoto
Originally published in Japan by Kodansha Ltd.
© 1998 English Edition by Heian International, Inc. USA

Translated by Dianne Ooka
Edited by Charisse Vega, Lisa Melton, and Monique Leahey Sugimoto

First American Edition 1999
99 00 01 02 03 04 05 10 9 8 7 6 5 4 3 2 1

HEIAN INTERNATIONAL, INC.
1815 West 205th Street, Suite #301
Torrance, CA 90501
Web Site : www.heian.com
E-mail: heianemail@heian.com

ISBN: 0-89346-849-5

Web site: www.heian.com
E-mail: heianemail@heian.com

Printed in Hong Kong

Table of Contents

VOLUME 2

The Straw Millionaire

Once upon a time there was a very poor, kind-hearted, hard-working young man. He was so poor that he decided to pray to the goddess of a nearby shrine. For twenty-one days in a row, he went to the shrine and prayed, "Please help me."

On the morning of the twenty-second day, the goddess appeared before him!

"Take good care of the very first thing you pick up today," she said. The young man was so happy that he jumped up and ran out of the shrine. He was in such a hurry that he fell flat on his face.

When he got up, he realized that he was holding on to a stalk of rice. "Well now...this is the first thing I have picked up today, so I have to take care of it," he said. He continued down the steps of the shrine, and soon a big black horsefly began to buzz around him.

So he caught the fly and tied it to the stalk. Then he tied the straw to a little twig that he found, and continued on his way with the horsefly like a little buzzing pet.

Soon he met a lady and her little boy. The boy saw the horsefly, and he began to beg for it. The young man was happy to give the fly to the boy. To thank him, the boy's mother gave him three juicy oranges.

The young man walked on. Next he met a beautiful, elegant young lady who was sitting by the side of the road. "Do you know where I can get some water?" she asked. "I'm so very, very thirsty!"

"Here, have these oranges," said the young man, and he handed them to her. The young lady was so grateful that she gave him a beautiful bolt of silk.

As the young man walked along, carrying his fine silk, he met a samurai on a magnificent stallion. Just as he got near the horse, it suddenly collapsed. The samurai and his servants all tried to get the horse to stand again, but the horse just laid on the road.

Finally the samurai gave up and asked a nearby farmer to lend him a horse. As he rode off, the young man spoke to the servant who was left behind to dispose of the horse. "What a shame—he's such a fine handsome animal!"

The servant replied, "This horse cost a lot of money. Now he's worthless." The young man felt sorry for the horse and said, "I'll give you this beautiful silk cloth if you'll let me have him!"

"Okay," agreed the servant. "He's all yours!" And he ran off down the road, happily carrying the silken cloth.

The young man stared at the horse, wishing that he could bring it back to life. He began to pray to the goddess of the shrine again. "Please, please dear Goddess...please help this poor horse!"

And then it happened! The horse jumped up and began to whinny.

"You're alive! You're alive!" cried the young man, and he jumped for joy.

The young man led the horse down the road. Soon he came to a huge farmhouse. The people who lived there were moving, and furniture and boxes were piled up outside. The master of the house saw the young man and said, "What a handsome horse! Would you take my house in return for your horse?"

The young man was amazed. The master bowed to him saying, "I must move to a faraway land, and I will not be coming back. The horse would be such a great help! I'll give you my rice fields and vegetable farm as well. Please let me have him!"

The young man happily handed the horse over. "Gosh...that first stalk of rice has turned into a mansion!", he marveled. "The goddess of the shrine has truly answered my prayers!"

Over the following years, he worked very hard, and soon he was very wealthy. Everyone called him "The Straw Millionaire!"

The Contest

Once upon a time there was a fox named Ohana and a badger named Gonbei. Each thought they were the best in the world at changing their appearance. One day when they met on a mountain path, they challenged each other to a contest.

Ohana immediately turned into a beautiful young bride—this was her favorite disguise. She was so lovely that no one who saw her would ever believe that she was really a fox! Just like a real bride, she looked shyly down at the ground as she daintily made her way to the nearby shrine.

As Ohana walked along, she saw a plump golden cake sitting on the path.

"Mmmm, that sure looks good!" thought Ohana as she began to drool. "I have enough time to eat the cake before that old Gonbei arrives!" And Ohana quickly picked up the cake and opened her mouth to take a big bite.

Suddenly, the cake turned into Gonbei, the badger!

"Ha, ha, ha," laughed Gonbei. "No matter how beautiful a bride you may have become, you are still a greedy little fox!"

Ohana was so embarrassed that she scampered off into the forest without saying a word!

The Bouncing Rice Ball

Once upon a time an old man and old woman lived in the forest. One day the old man went to gather firewood in the nearby mountains. For his lunch he took some rice balls that his wife had made.

At noon, the old man sat down to eat the rice balls. As he unwrapped them, one of the rice balls fell and began rolling along. Soon it disappeared down a hole in the ground.

The old man chased after the rice ball, and when he peered down the hole, he heard sweet little voices singing a song.

"Bounce, little rice ball...bounce, bounce, bounce...
For ever and ever let no cat meow!"

"Hmmm...that's strange," said the old man. And just then, he fell into the hole.

When he got to the bottom, he saw a lovely palace. The singing mice had taken the rice ball and were busily pounding the rice to make rice cakes!

"What a surprise!" marveled the old man.

The mice came to him and said, "Thank you so much for the rice ball. But, old man, please don't ever talk about cats. We hate cats!"

Of course I won't say anything...why would I even want to?" asked the old man. The mice happily served him a feast fit for a king, and he ate to his heart's content.

Then he decided to head home, the mice brought him a woven straw purse filled with gold coins. "Close your eyes," they said.

The old man closed his eyes, and *abracadabra!* He found himself back at the entrance to the hole! The old man carried the purse home and told everyone about his good fortune.

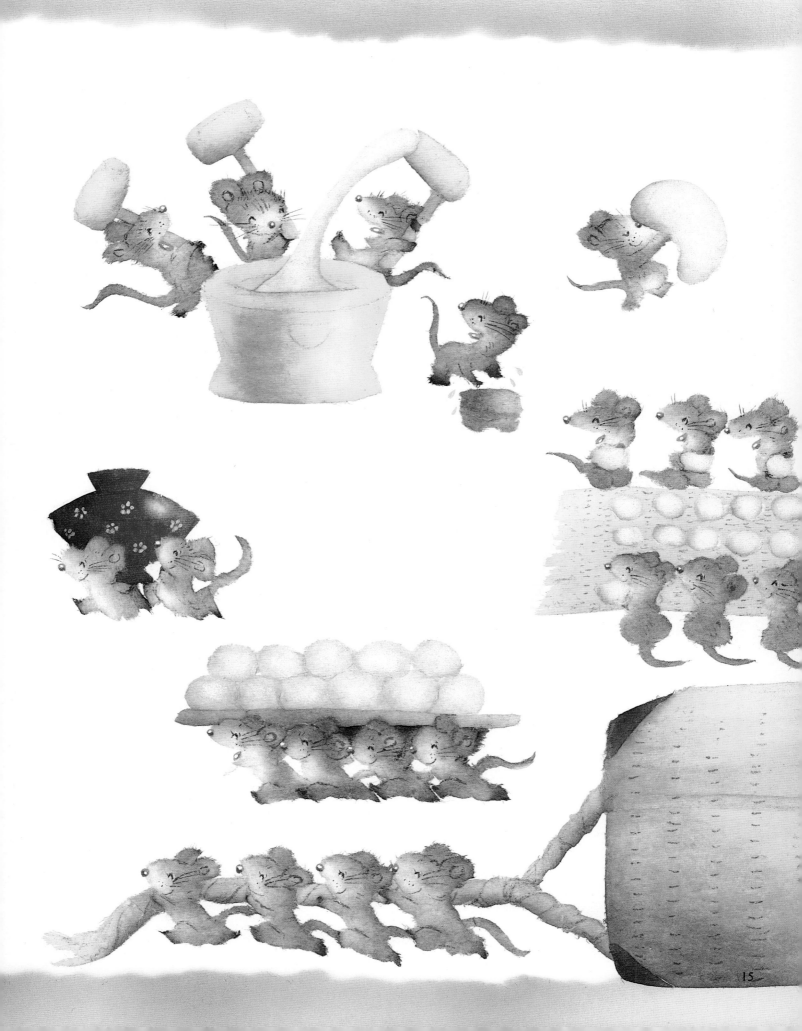

Next door lived a greedy old man. He became jealous when he heard about his neighbor's good fortune. He quickly had his wife make some rice balls, then headed out for the mountain. He looked high and low for the hole and soon found it. He threw a rice ball down the hole and then jumped in right after it.

When he got to the bottom of the hole, he saw the mouse palace. There were the mice dancing in a circle and, at the entrance to the palace, were piled all kinds of treasures and baskets filled with gold coins.

The mice came to the old man and said, "Thank you so very much for the rice ball. But, old man please don't talk about cats. We hate cats!"

The greedy old man thought to himself, "Hmmm...maybe if I were to meow like a cat, they'd all be so scared that they would run away. Then I can take all those treasures home, and I'll be rich!"

So the greedy old man began. "Meow! Meow!", he mewed, and all the mice ran away. But at the same time, everything turned pitch black.

The old man couldn't find his way out of the hole, and he had to live underground forever, unable to see anything again.

The Monkeys' Statue

Long ago, an old man went to work in his rice field on the mountainside. It was such a beautiful day that he decided to lie down and enjoy the sun. Soon he fell asleep. Along came a large band of monkeys.

"Look here! A statue has fallen on the path! If we don't carry it to the temple, we'll all be in trouble."

The old man heard the monkeys talking and was very surprised. Who ever heard monkeys talk? However, he thought it would be fun to be a statue, so he pretended to still be asleep.

The monkeys all lifted the old man up and carried him above their heads.

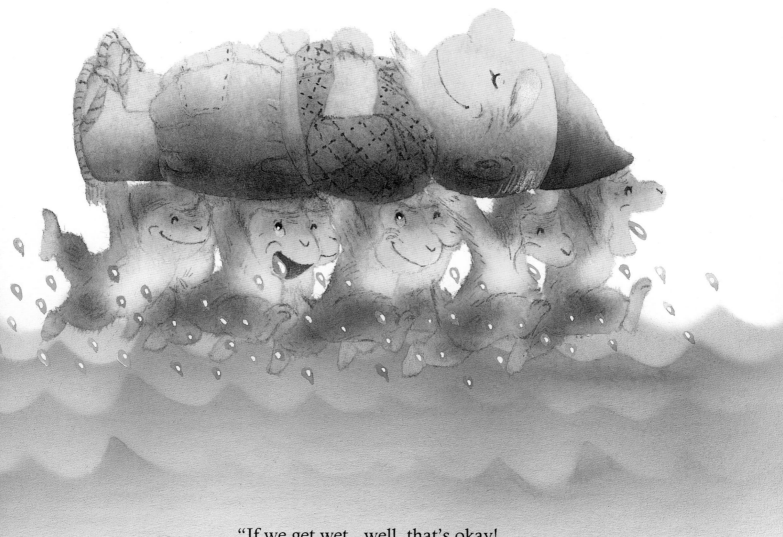

"If we get wet...well, that's okay!
Let the statue get wet? No, no way!"

This was the refrain that the monkeys sang happily as they forded the river. The old man thought it was so funny—he was being tickled and wanted to laugh out loud! But he managed to stay still and not make a sound.

On the other side of the river was a little temple. The monkeys placed the old man reverently inside the temple and brought many gifts. The old man stayed very still, pretending to be a statue.

When the monkeys left, the old man opened his eyes. There were cakes and fruits everywhere! He happily carried them back to his home.

When he returned home, he told the neighbors about his good fortune.
A greedy old man heard his story. The very next day he headed for the
rice field in the mountains and laid down on one of the paths.

And sure enough, along came the same large band of monkeys.

"Look, here's another statue! If we don't carry him back to the temple,
we'll get in trouble," said the monkeys. Together the monkeys lifted
the old man and carried him above their heads.

"If we get wet...well, that's okay!
Let the statue get wet? No, no way!"

Singing loudly, the monkeys splashed through the river. The old man thought it was really funny—he felt like he was being tickled by the monkeys carrying him, and so he finally started to laugh.

"Ha, ha, ha, ha...!"

At that, the monkeys stopped in surprise.

"This isn't a statue!" they cried, and they threw the old man into the river and ran away.

Little One Inch Boy

Once upon a time there lived an old man and old woman who had no children. They went to the shrine every day and prayed, "Please, please...let us have a child!" Then one day a child was born to them. The strange thing was that this child was no bigger than the old man's little finger.

"This child must be a gift from the gods," said the old couple, and they named him Little One Inch Boy. But Little One Inch Boy never grew any taller in the years that followed, and his parents worried about him.

One day, when he had become a man, Little One Inch Boy announced to his parents, "I'm going to the capital city!"

Although they didn't want him to leave, his parents gave him permission for his journey. His father made him a sword out of a sewing needle, and his mother gave him a soup bowl and chopstick to use as a boat and oar.

Wearing his sword on his side, Little One Inch Boy set off downstream in his little soup bowl.

Several days later, Little One Inch Boy arrived in the city. He walked through the streets and came to a grand mansion. He stood at the gate and cried in a loud voice, "I am Little One Inch Boy! I would like to serve the master of this house!"

The samurai master came to the front gate to see who was calling. He saw Little One Inch Boy standing on a wooden sandal.

"Well now, aren't you an interesting little fellow," said the samurai. He took a liking to the lad and kindly allowed Little One Inch Boy to join his household.

Little One Inch Boy was small but he was very smart. Soon everyone in the samurai's household loved him—and the samurai's daughter, Little Princess, loved him best of all.

One day Little One Inch Boy went with the princess and her servants to the local shrine. On the way home, they were attacked by two ogres—one red and one blue. The ogres tried to kidnap the princess.

"Stop!" cried Little One Inch Boy as he jumped out of the princess' sash with his sword drawn.

"Ho, ho, ho...what's this? Look at this little shrimp," laughed the red ogre. He picked Little One Inch Boy up and swallowed him in one gulp.

But once inside, Little One Inch Boy began to run around the red ogre's stomach, poking everywhere with his sword.

"Ouch, ouch, ouch!" cried the red ogre. He spat Little One Inch Boy out and held his stomach.

Little One Inch Boy landed on the blue ogre's face. He started to prick the ogre's eyes with his sword, and soon both ogres ran away, crying in pain.

The princess picked up the mallet that the ogre had dropped. She had heard that ogres carry magic mallets, so she began to wave it back and forth. The princess began to chant, "Grow, Little One Inch Boy, grow nice and tall!"

And *abracadabra*—Little One Inch Boy began to grow. Right before her eyes, he became a handsome young man!

The master was so pleased with Little One Inch Boy's bravery that he asked Little One Inch Boy to marry the princess. Little One Inch Boy then brought his parents to the city—and everyone lived happily ever after.

27

Tail Fishing

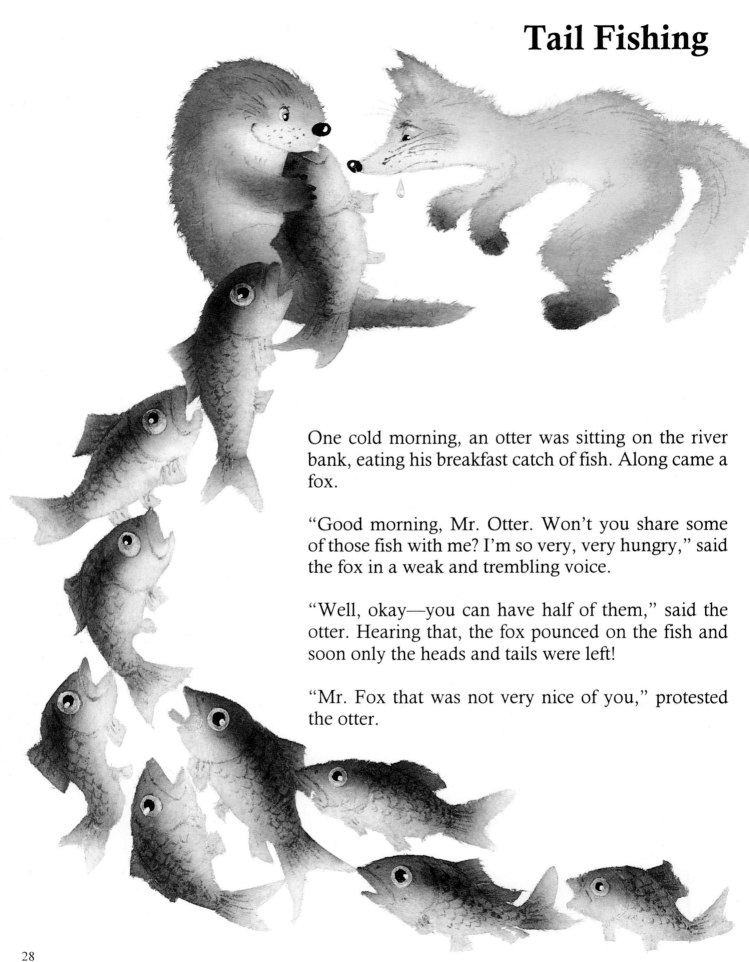

One cold morning, an otter was sitting on the river bank, eating his breakfast catch of fish. Along came a fox.

"Good morning, Mr. Otter. Won't you share some of those fish with me? I'm so very, very hungry," said the fox in a weak and trembling voice.

"Well, okay—you can have half of them," said the otter. Hearing that, the fox pounced on the fish and soon only the heads and tails were left!

"Mr. Fox that was not very nice of you," protested the otter.

But the fox just laid back without any shame and said,
"By the way, Mr. Otter. How do you catch such
delicious fish?"

The otter was so angry that he wanted to get even with
the fox. He thought for a moment and then replied,
"It's really easy. All you have to do is sit on the bank
of the river until morning with your tail in the water.
The fish will come, think your tail is bait, and bite
onto it!"

"I see," said the fox. "That sounds nice and easy!"

That night, the fox sat on the river bank and lowered his tail into the water. It was really cold, but he sat there patiently. He couldn't wait to eat more delicious fish again! He noticed that his tail was getting heavier and heavier.

"Hmmm...I must be catching alot of fish," thought the fox happily. He didn't even notice that the river was beginning to freeze.

The night finally ended and the sun began to rise.

"Well, guess it is time for me to pull in the fish," said the fox. But no matter how hard he pulled, his tail was stuck—it was frozen solid in the river!

Just then, a farmer came by.

"Hey...there's that naughty fox who's been bothering my animals! Now I can trap him," cried the farmer.

Hearing that, the fox was so scared that he gave a great pull. His tail broke in half with a loud snap, and he ran into the forest, squealing in pain.

The otter had gotten his revenge!

A NOTE TO PARENTS:
Capturing a Child's Imagination

Children are just full of curiosity. They're always looking about expectantly, wanting to discover new things. The more they learn, the wider their eyes open to find what interests them.

A child's interest in books begin with wordless picture books, then turns to picture books with stories. Though some children may read and interpret these storybooks on their own, most must rely on an adult to help read and interpret the stories for them. During this important period of development, it is critical for children to have stories read aloud to them by an adult. A child's mother and father are the adults who are the closest and most dear to the child. Indeed, hearing the loving voice of a mother or father telling (and retelling) a story can become one of the child's most reassuring memories. In addition, by reading stories aloud, parents enrich their child's imagination. Just as food provides nutrition for the child's growing body, the interchange between child and parent during storytelling can be a nutrient for the mind and soul.

The collection of stories in this volume include some of Japan's most cherished tales. As with all fables and legends, it isn't clear where, by whom, or even when these stories were composed. Most likely, the tales grew out of the daily lives of our ancestors and from generation to generation, were passed from parent to child. What is clear about the fairy tales, however, is their value. Whose imagination wouldn't be captivated by shape-shifting animals, a one-inch-tall warrior, a band of singing mice, and other stories of the fantastic? But the *Japanese Fairy Tales* are more than just entertaining; they also address some of life's enduring themes: How to live a good, kind life; how to achieve happiness; and the price to be paid for cruelty, greediness, and cowardice. Through these tales, then, and through the humorous way in which they are told, children learn human virtue and traditional wisdom.

Keisuke Nishimoto, Professor
Showa Woman's College
Tokyo, Japan